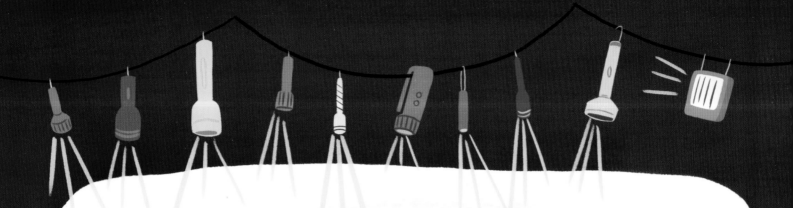

For Melissa Savage, friend of all things
that go bump in the night. —D. R.

To a lady who always supports me and who has loved these
characters from the first sight: my sister, my beloved Paula.
Best friend and guide, one of the loves of my life.
I will always try to hug you twice. —I. M.

Henry Holt and Company, *Publishers since 1866*
Henry Holt® is a registered trademark of Macmillan Publishing Group, LLC
120 Broadway, New York, NY 10271 • mackids.com

ISBN 978-1-250-20934-4
Library of Congress Control Number 2019949517

Our books may be purchased in bulk for promotional, educational, or business use.
Please contact your local bookseller or the Macmillan Corporate and Premium Sales Department
at (800) 221-7945 ext. 5442 or by email at MacmillanSpecialMarkets@macmillan.com.

First edition, 2020 / Design by Mike Burroughs and Sophie Erb
The illustrations for this book were created digitally.
Printed in China by Hung Hing Off-set Printing Co. Ltd., Heshan City, Guangdong Province

1 3 5 7 9 10 8 6 4 2

BUTTERCUP
THE BIGFOOT

ILLUSTRATED BY

DOUGLAS REES ISABEL MUÑOZ

HENRY HOLT ☾ NEW YORK

Willa Cathcart Wilmerding was the bravest little girl in the world. She climbed the tallest trees.

She swam in the
deepest waters.

She petted the
meanest dogs.

She even liked spiders.

Willa was good in school.

She could spell

H·E·L·I·C·O·P·T·E·R

and play the oboe
in the orchestra.

She was in Scouts. She had 326 merit badges.

And on Friday nights, Willa liked to climb up on the roof and HOWL at the moon all night long.

AAAAA-OO

"Willa, you must calm down and stop
howling on the roof," her mother told her.
"It is time to concentrate on school and Scouts."

So Willa decided to go someplace where her mother couldn't hear her. She packed her bag and went to the mountains.

High in the mountains
lived a Bigfoot. She loved to
scare hikers. She would leap out
of her hiding place and roar and show
her fangs and stomp her huge feet.
Then she would howl.

AAAAA-OOOOO-EeeEE-YAAAH!

The hikers would drop their gear and run.
The Bigfoot would take it all home and decorate with it.

High up on the steepest peak, Willa reached the Bigfoot's favorite scaring place. The Bigfoot leaped out and screeched:

Willa smiled.

she said.

The Bigfoot snarled and waved her long, strong arms.
She jumped up and down so hard, she almost shook the mountain.

"I like you," Willa said. "You've got big feet."
Then she went:

Finally, the Bigfoot bent over Willa and wiggled her sharp claws.
She growled and showed her fangs.

Willa threw back her head and howled her favorite howl:

The Bigfoot just stood there.
"What's your name?" Willa said.

"Rrrrrrrrrr,"
the Bigfoot said.

"Your name is
Buttercup, okay?"
Willa said.

The Bigfoot nodded.

"I'm getting cold," Willa said.
So Buttercup picked Willa up and
carried her back to her cave.

"What a lovely home," Willa said. "Let's play house.
You be the baby, and I'll be the mommy."

"Rrrrrrr?" said Buttercup.
"I'll teach you," Willa said.

Willa gave Buttercup a bath.

Then she combed and brushed all her long hair.
When Willa was done, Buttercup felt wonderful.

"You're a good baby,"
Willa said.

That night,
they slept cuddled
together, warm
and happy.

Willa and Buttercup did everything together.
They leaped up and down the mountains.

They soared over mighty crevasses.

They made each other
crowns of flowers.

But their favorite thing of all was to climb up on a high peak and HOWL at the moon all night long.

AAA-OOO-E
AAA-OOO-E

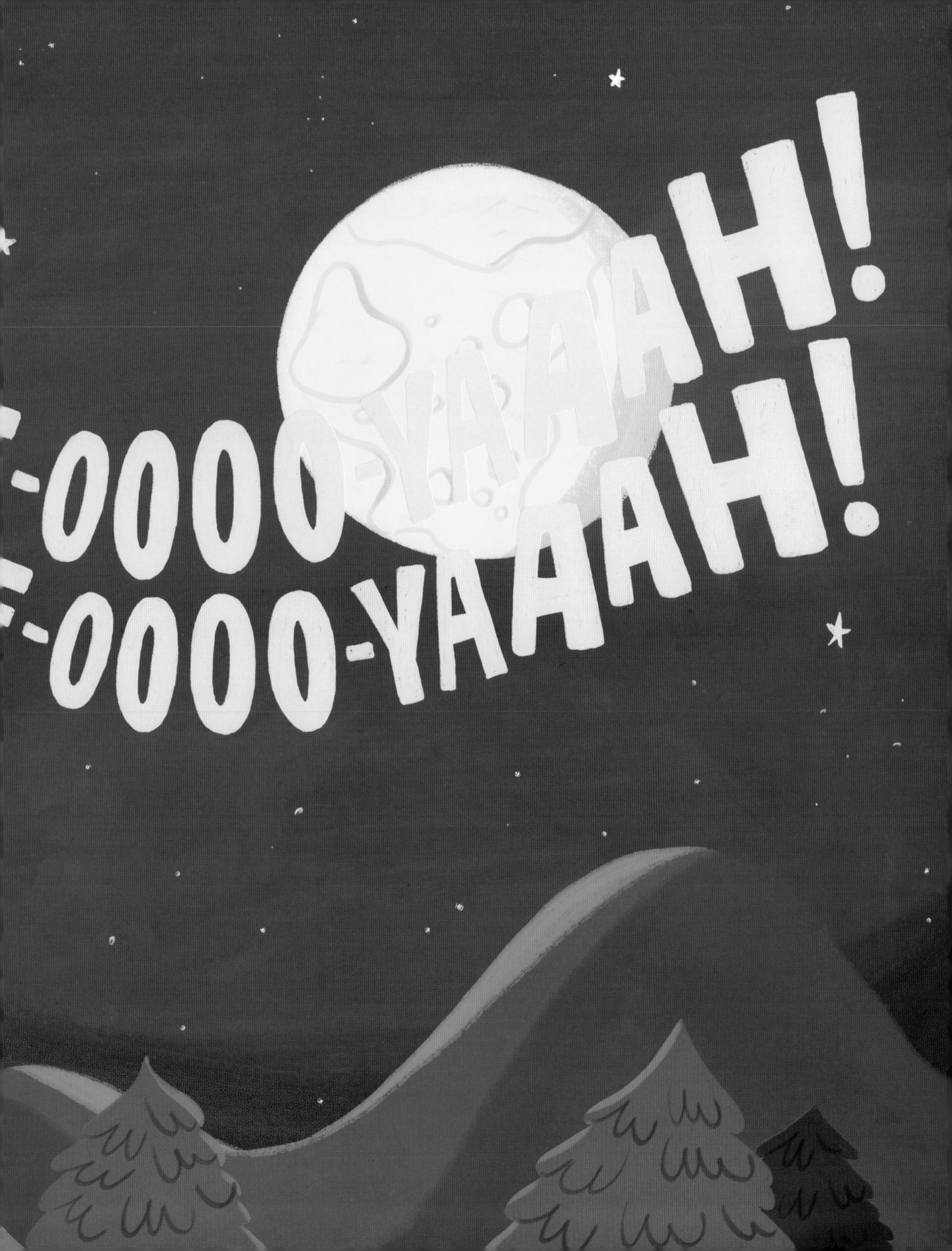

-OOOO-YAAAH!
-OOOO-YAAAAH!

One day, a helicopter landed. Willa's mother got out.
"Willa, I miss you," she said. "It's time for
you to go back to school and Scouts."

"Can Buttercup come, too?" Willa asked.
"I'm afraid not," Willa's mother said. "It's a small helicopter."

Willa hugged Buttercup.
"Don't forget how to play house," Willa said.

Buttercup sadly
waved goodbye.

Willa went back to school. She played eight new pieces on the oboe, and she earned twenty-seven more merit badges. But she missed Buttercup.

One Friday night, when she was softly howling to herself,
she heard something. It was coming closer and closer.

It was Buttercup, bounding over the rooftops!
They hugged. "I've been so lonely," Willa said.

Buttercup likes being a little girl.
She's learned to divide and how to spell *Rrrrr*.

In the school orchestra, she plays the tuba.

She even goes to Scouts.
She won a merit badge for her flower
arrangements. Everything is fine.

And every Friday night, Buttercup and Willa climb
up on the roof and HOWL at the moon all night long.